This Little Tiger book belongs to:

To Deborah Prince and Charles Lilley,
with thanks
~ C F

For Sue, you have helped me realise
so many dreams. Thank you
~ D H

LITTLE TIGER PRESS LTD,
an imprint of the Little Tiger Group
1 Coda Studios, 189 Munster Road,
London SW6 6AW
www.littletiger.co.uk

First published in Great Britain 2004
This edition published 2018

Text copyright © Claire Freedman 2004
Illustrations copyright © Daniel Howarth 2004
Claire Freedman and Daniel Howarth have
asserted their rights to be identified as the author
and illustrator of this work under the Copyright,
Designs and Patents Act, 1988
All rights reserved

ISBN 978-1-78881-176-7
A CIP catalogue record for this book is available
from the British Library
Printed in China • LTP/1800/2323/0818

2 4 6 8 10 9 7 5 3 1

The Busy Busy Day

Claire Freedman   Daniel Howarth

LiTTLE TiGER
LONDON

"Hooray! Spring is here!" cried Ginger, tugging on his old boots. "Come on, Floppy, let's go and do some gardening."

They marched outside and looked around.

"What shall we do first, Ginger?" asked Floppy excitedly.

"I know!" said Ginger. "Let's clear away those logs." And he went to get the wheelbarrow.

CHIRP! CHIRP! CHIRP!

Two worried-looking robins swooped down.

"Hmmm, something's bothering them," said Ginger. "I can't see anything wrong, can you?"

"No!" said Floppy, shaking his head. "Perhaps they think we want to eat their worms!"

They looked in the wheelbarrow and couldn't believe their eyes. Snug in one corner lay a nestful of baby robins!

CHEEP! CHEEP! CHEEP!

"So that's why the robins were chirping," said Ginger. "They thought we might frighten their baby chicks. We mustn't disturb them."

"What shall we do now, Ginger?" Floppy asked.

"Hmm," said Ginger thoughtfully. "Well, we can't clear away the logs without a wheelbarrow. We'll do another job instead."

They started to pick up the flowerpots and stack them.

Oh! Now Ginger had found something else. "Come and look at this, Floppy," he whispered. "But be very, very quiet!"

Inside the biggest flowerpot two tiny hedgehogs were curled up, fast asleep. They snuffled and snored noisily.

"Oooh!" gasped Floppy excitedly. "Don't they look funny!"

"Shhh, don't say a word!" Ginger hushed. "We mustn't wake them!"

They both tiptoed away without a sound.

"Well, Floppy," said Ginger. "We can't sort out the flowerpots. But there are still lots of other jobs we can do."

He opened the shed door. "We can tidy up in here," he said.

EEEK! EEEK! EEEK!

"That's not the door creaking," said Ginger. "Is it you making that funny noise, Floppy?"

"No!" Floppy giggled. "Maybe your old boots are squeaking, Ginger."

"It's not me *or* my boots," Ginger replied. "So what can it be?"

Floppy peered along the dusty shelves between the boxes and baskets.

"Atchoo!" he sneezed.

Ginger checked the bulb packets. Floppy tipped the watering can upside down.

Nothing!

EEEK! EEEK!

"There it goes again, Floppy!" said Ginger. "What is it?"

"I don't know," said Floppy. "But it's a *very* loud squeak!"

Ginger sat down by some seed trays to think
what it could be…and very nearly squashed
a family of mice!

"Goodness, that was close!" said Ginger.
"So *that's* what was squeaking! Well, we can't
tidy up the shed now. We might disturb
the mice!"

Ginger closed the shed door quietly behind them.

"Don't worry, Floppy!" he said. "We can still do the weeding. All those dandelions must go!"

Floppy kneeled beside the flowerbeds. A big orange butterfly landed on his nose.

"Hee hee!" laughed Floppy. "That tickles!"

Another butterfly fluttered around Floppy's ears.

"Aha!" Ginger said to Floppy. "I think the butterflies are trying to tell us something!"

"What could that be?" said Floppy in surprise.

Ginger looked closely at the dandelion leaves.

"Just as I thought," he said. "Caterpillars! One day they'll grow into butterflies too. No more weeding till then!"

Ginger and Floppy walked back up the garden.
Ginger pulled off his old boots.

"Our garden may not be tidy," he said, looking
around, "but I think it's perfect just the way it is!"

"You're right, Ginger," Floppy agreed happily.

"It's perfect for all

our little friends and . . .

"…it's just perfect for a sunny picnic too!"

Ginger fetched the picnic blanket. Floppy brought out some orangeade and cakes.

"Everyone can enjoy our garden," Ginger said cheerfully as he tucked in.

And everyone did!